Play time

Catherine and Laurence Anholt

little ORCHARD

Would you like to play with me?

this

little ORCHARD

book belongs to

....

....

For Daniel

ORCHARD BOOKS
96 Leonard Street, London EC2A 4XD
Orchard Books Australia
14 Mars Road, Lane Cove, NSW 2066
1 83069 189 3 (hardback)
1 84121 307 1 (paperback)
First published in Great Britain in 1999
Copyright text © Laurence Anholt 1999
Copyright illustrations © Catherine Anholt 1999
The rights of Laurence Anholt to be identified as the author and Catherine Anholt
as the illustrator of this work have been asserted by them in accordance
with the Copyright, Designs and Patents Act, 1988.
A CIP catalogue record for this book is available from the British Library.
Printed in Italy

Share the biscuits, picnic tea?

Look down at the world below.

Hurry up now, don't be slow.

Yellow paint, and red and green.

You'll be king and I'll be queen.

Take our teddies for a ride.

Can you find me if I hide?

Banging, crashing, what a noise!

Watching quietly with my toys.

We are building in the snow.

I can cycle, watch me go!

Hop and skip and leap and jump.

Climb and hold and slide and bump.

We are dancing, come and look.

Snuggle up close, share a book.